DreamWorks
SHREK

DREAMWORKS
PRESS
Los Angeles · New York

Written by K. Emily Hutta ★ Illustrated by Ovi Nedelcu
Published by DreamWorks Press, 1000 Flower Street, Glendale, California 91201. ★ Printed in China
2 4 6 8 10 9 7 5 3 1
09112015-F-1 ★ ISBN 978-1-941341-80-3
Visit dreamworkspress.com

ar, far away—in a land full of weird and wonderful fairy tale creatures—there lived a cranky, crusty, stupendously stinky ogre named Shrek.

Shrek's home-not-so-sweet-home sat in a stinky swamp many miles from the nearest neighbor. No one ever came to visit because ogres really did not like company.

So Shrek spent his days alone. Which was just the way he wanted it.

Late one afternoon, Shrek was out in the forest when—*thump*—a peculiar little four-legged beast crashed right into him.

To Shrek's utter amazement, the beast started to talk. And talk. And talk some more.

The ogre didn't know what to do. So he roared and glared and did his ogre-ish best to scare the pesky fellow away.

But Donkey still followed him home.

For an ogre who liked his privacy, having one houseguest was bad enough. But when a whole group of unruly fairy tale guests suddenly showed up, Shrek lost his cool.

"WHAT ARE YOU DOING IN MY SWAMP?" the outraged ogre bellowed.

Donkey just shrugged. "I didn't invite them," he said.

The new arrivals weren't any happier to be in Shrek's swamp than he was to have them there. But Lord Farquaad, the ruler of DuLoc, had chased all the fairy tale creatures out of his kingdom.

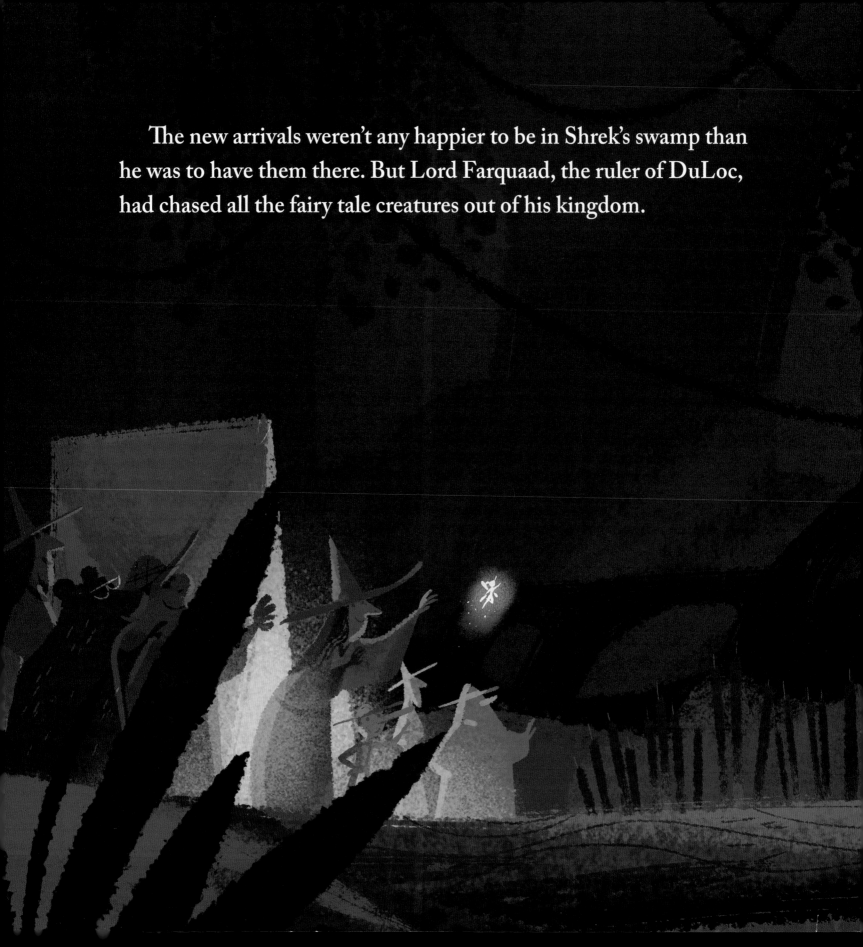

So the ogre set out to find this fellow who was messing with his perfectly peaceful privacy.

Donkey cheerfully tagged along.

Shrek and Donkey arrived in DuLoc right in the middle of Lord Farquaad's grand tournament.

The knights were about to battle each other when Farquaad spotted Shrek. He ordered his knights to fight Shrek instead. But they were no match for the ogre.

Shrek's prize for winning the tournament was to complete a dangerous quest to rescue Lord Farquaad's future fiancee, Princess Fiona. It was the only way Shrek would get his swamp back and have any peace and privacy again.

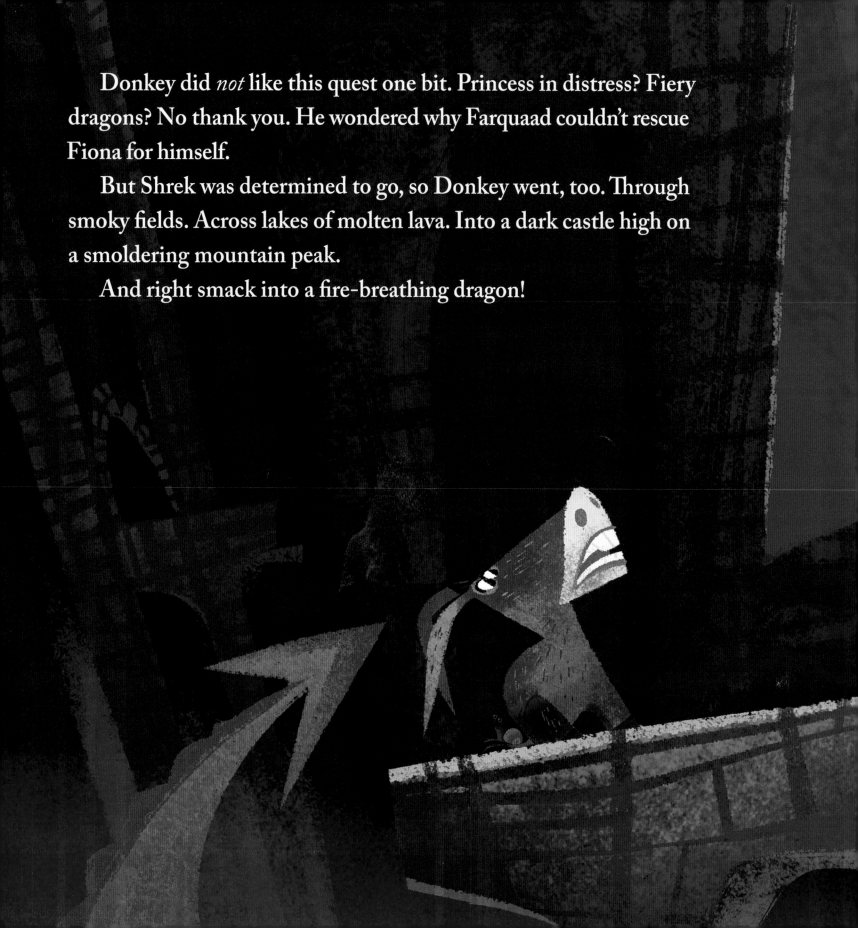

Donkey did *not* like this quest one bit. Princess in distress? Fiery dragons? No thank you. He wondered why Farquaad couldn't rescue Fiona for himself.

But Shrek was determined to go, so Donkey went, too. Through smoky fields. Across lakes of molten lava. Into a dark castle high on a smoldering mountain peak.

And right smack into a fire-breathing dragon!

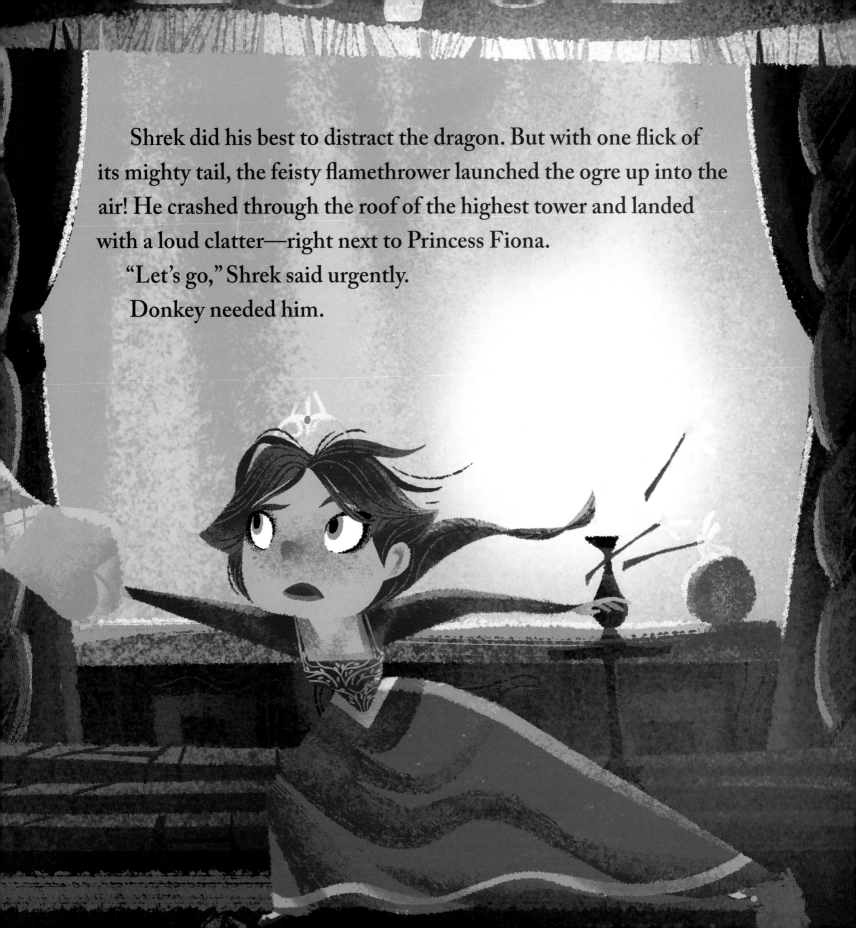

Shrek did his best to distract the dragon. But with one flick of its mighty tail, the feisty flamethrower launched the ogre up into the air! He crashed through the roof of the highest tower and landed with a loud clatter—right next to Princess Fiona.

"Let's go," Shrek said urgently.

Donkey needed him.

Shrek hurried downstairs to save his friend. But Donkey had already won over the dragon. The dragon had a crush on Donkey—and she really didn't want to let him go.

Shrek was in no mood to argue. He grabbed Donkey with one arm and Fiona with the other. They dashed from the castle with the disappointed dragon hot on their heels.

Princess Fiona was not at all happy with the way her fairy tale rescue was going. Shrek was on a noble quest to save—not her—but his stinky swamp. Meanwhile, Lord Farquaad, her supposed Prince Charming, was lounging around in his castle waiting for Fiona.

Worst of all, the princess would have to wait until they arrived in DuLoc for love's first kiss to break her secret spell.

The journey to DuLoc was long and filled with surprises.

Shrek had never met anyone like Fiona before. This princess knew karate and wasn't afraid of bugs. She burped like a champion. She even enjoyed his roasted weedrat recipe!

The more Shrek got to know Fiona, the more he liked her. But how could the princess possibly feel the same way about a big green ogre like him.

Surprisingly, Fiona had begun to enjoy Shrek's company, too.
But she didn't think he could possibly feel the same way. So...
with her newly found escort, Lord Farquaad, Fiona continued
on to DuLoc.

And Shrek stomped off to his swamp *alone*.

Convinced that his friends were fools for not talking things out,
Donkey decided to save the day.

When Donkey returned to Shrek's swamp, Dragon was with him.
Donkey figured if he could befriend a fiery dragon, he could surely
persuade a stubborn, stinky ogre to save a certain princess. Again.

Shrek realized that he had made a terrible mistake. He had to tell
Fiona how he felt before she married Lord Farquaad.

Dragon flew her new friends across the countryside toward
DuLoc. But would they get there in time?

Fiona was in a panic. Fairy tale or no fairy tale, she didn't believe that Farquaad was her true love. And if the sun set before she received love's first kiss, her secret would be revealed to the entire kingdom.

Shrek burst into the cathedral just as the sun's last rays faded from the sky. At that moment, Fiona was surrounded by a dazzling light. When the light faded, a beautiful green ogress appeared!

"Well, that explains a lot," Shrek said.

Lord Farquaad was horrified. He wanted a picture-perfect princess for his picture-perfect kingdom. Fiona wouldn't do at all.

Shrek had never been happier. Maybe Fiona *could* love a big green ogre like him after all. Maybe he was her Prince Charming!

When Fiona kissed Shrek, she once again disappeared in a brilliant shower of light. The spell was finally broken! Fiona would no longer have to transform from a princess into an ogress each night.

As the light faded once again, the crowd gasped. Standing where Fiona the ogress had been was ... Fiona the ogress!

"I don't understand," Fiona said. She had always thought that when the spell was broken, she would be a princess forever. "I'm supposed to be beautiful."

"But you are beautiful," Shrek said.

Donkey nodded in agreement.

The day Shrek and Fiona were married, the swamp overflowed with weird and wonderful fairy tale creatures. Only this time, they had all been invited!

On a quest to protect his peace and privacy, Shrek had found true love and true friendship instead.

And, oh how Donkey talked about it—and talked about it—and talked about it—*chattily* ever after.

Sweet dreams!